BIGFOOT CINDERRRRRELLA

BY TONY JOHNSTON

ILLUSTRATED BY JAMES WARHOLA

G. P. PUTNAM'S SONS • NEW YORK

BIGFOOT CINDERRRRRELLA GLOSSARY

Banana slug: California state mollusk

Bigfoot: Legendary huge, hairy, humanlike creature said
to live in the Trinity Alps region of northern California;
also called Sasquatch; similiar to the fabled Yeti of
the Himalayas

Deadfall: Fallen tree

Douglas fir: Tree of the pine family

Hemlock: Tree of the pine family

Old-growth forest: Stand of trees 250 years old or more

Sapling: Young tree

Snag: Dead tree

Spotted owl: Endangered bird dwelling chiefly in old-growth
forests of California and the Pacific Northwest

Text copyright © 1998 by Tony Johnston

Illustrations copyright © 1998 by James Warhola

Printed in Hong Kong by South China Printing Co. (1988) Ltd.

Designed by Gunta Alexander. Text set in Breughel

Library of Congress Cataloging-in-Publication Data.
Johnston, Tony, 1942- Bigfoot Cinderrrrella/by Tony Johnston; illustrated by James Warhola
p. cm. Summary: This version of the familiar story in which a mistreated step-child finds
happiness with the "man" of her dreams is set in the old-growth forest and features Bigfoot
characters. [1. Fairy tales. 2. Folklore.] I. Warhola, James, ill. II. Title. PZ8.J494Bi 1998
398.2–dc21 97-47761 CIP AC ISBN 0-399-23021-1
10 9 8 7 6 5 4 3

For the California grizzly,
now extinct,
and all those who protect
the old-growth forest. —T. J.

For our lovely new daughter,
Oonagh. —J. W.

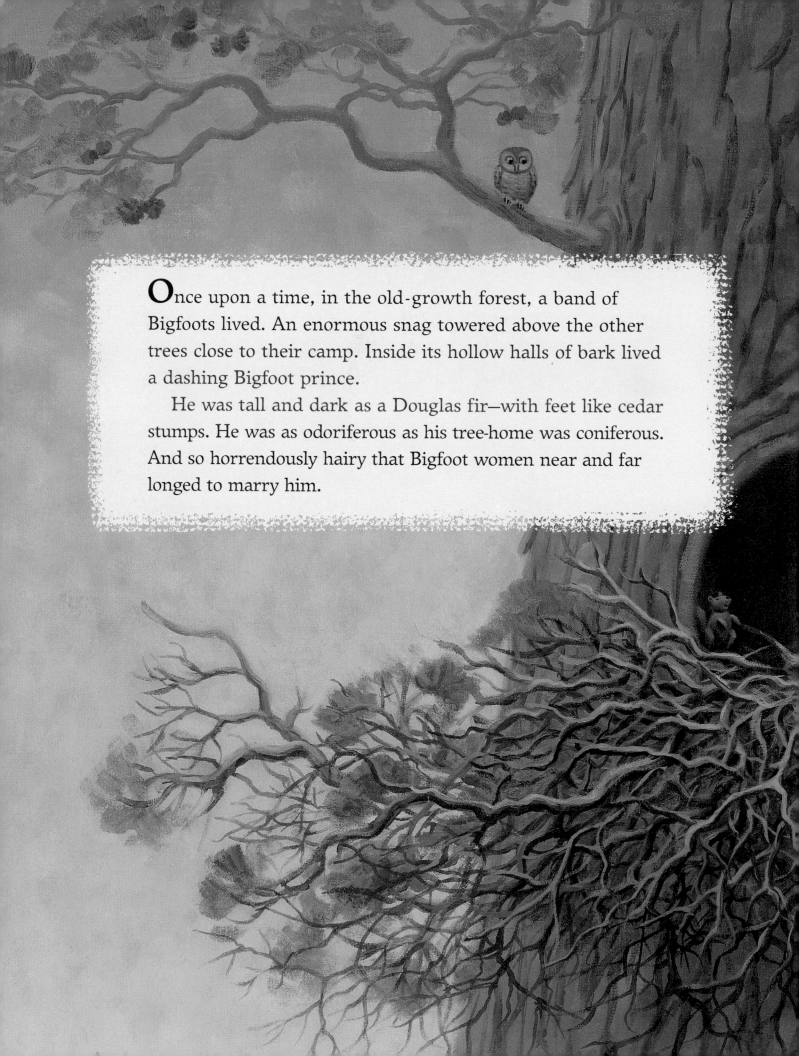

Once upon a time, in the old-growth forest, a band of Bigfoots lived. An enormous snag towered above the other trees close to their camp. Inside its hollow halls of bark lived a dashing Bigfoot prince.

He was tall and dark as a Douglas fir—with feet like cedar stumps. He was as odoriferous as his tree-home was coniferous. And so horrendously hairy that Bigfoot women near and far longed to marry him.

Whenever they saw him lurching along they blocked his
path like deadfalls. They draped wildflowers around themselves.
They batted their matted eyelashes, to stun him into love.

But the prince loved nature best.

"No pick flowers!" he bellowed at them in a voice as rough
as bark.

In this place there lived a Bigfoot woman and her three daughters. Well, really, only two were hers. The third was a stepchild.

The daughters were puny things with dinky feet, almost furless as Bigfoots go, and as sour as little green berries. They spent their days bathing and picking their teeth with fishbones and sleeking their fur with pinecones. For fun, they threw rocks at spotted owls.

The stepdaughter was just the opposite—nearly as woolly as a mammoth, golden as a banana slug, with feet like log canoes. She loved nature and would harm no creature.

Her stepsisters despised her and they made her work. Although her name was Ella, they roared at her so much that everyone called her Rrrrrella.

"*Rrrrrella, fix fire!*"

"*Rrrrrella, catch fish!*"

They forced her to comb her fur—and stick wildflowers in it! If she tugged them out, they put back twice as many!

In spite of this primping, Rrrrrella was sooty from the fire and stinking with fish. So they teased her like stinging mosquitos.

"You beast." They laughed and held their noses.

"You positive rrrrreek."

"*You absolute fffffreak!*"

Then they bathed her a lot in the creek.

"EEEEEK!"

One morning, Rrrrrella went to the river to get supper. She fished all day, and tossed her catch onto the bank in a silvery pile.

Suddenly, a grizzly bear appeared. He seemed hungry. Rrrrrella was bigger than the bear, so she could have shooed him away. But she was too kind. She let him have the fish.

When she shambled home empty-handed, her stepsisters rubbed their bellies and bellowed, *"Food! Food! Food!"* They forced her to fish all night.

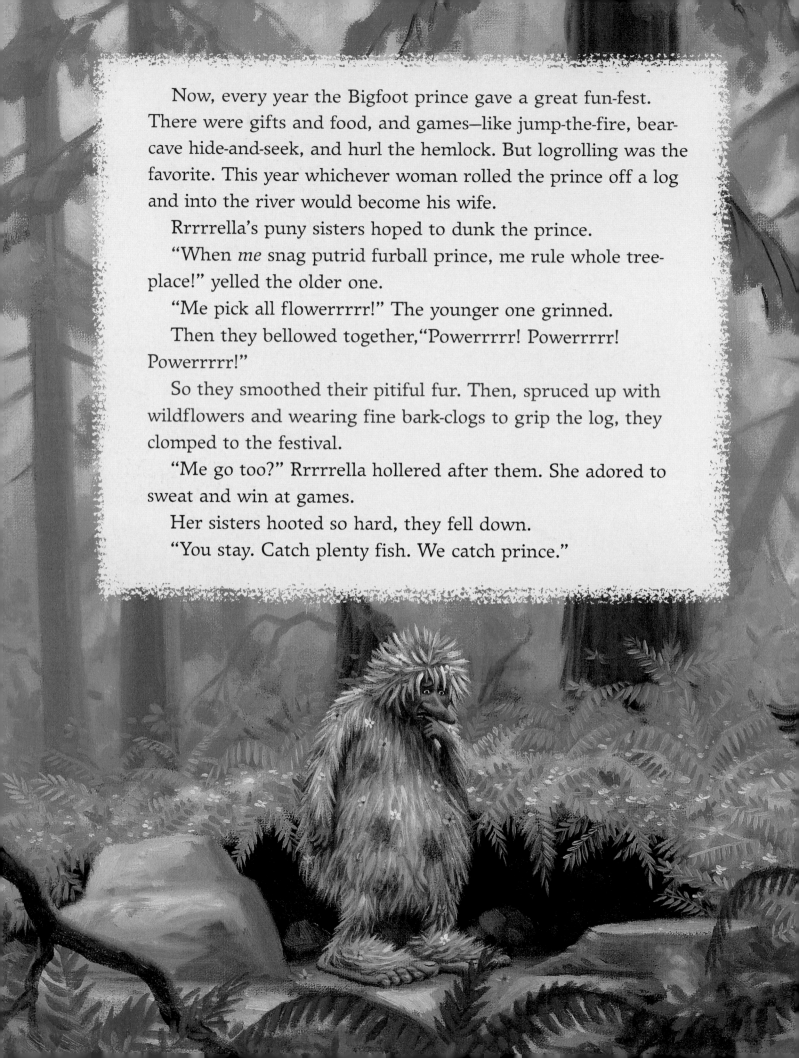

Now, every year the Bigfoot prince gave a great fun-fest. There were gifts and food, and games—like jump-the-fire, bear-cave hide-and-seek, and hurl the hemlock. But logrolling was the favorite. This year whichever woman rolled the prince off a log and into the river would become his wife.

Rrrrrella's puny sisters hoped to dunk the prince.

"When *me* snag putrid furball prince, me rule whole tree-place!" yelled the older one.

"Me pick all flowerrrrr!" The younger one grinned.

Then they bellowed together, "Powerrrrr! Powerrrrr! Powerrrrr!"

So they smoothed their pitiful fur. Then, spruced up with wildflowers and wearing fine bark-clogs to grip the log, they clomped to the festival.

"Me go too?" Rrrrrella hollered after them. She adored to sweat and win at games.

Her sisters hooted so hard, they fell down.

"You stay. Catch plenty fish. We catch prince."

How Rrrrrella longed to go! Sadly, she stared at the river. She saw a fish jump. She made a wish on the fish. "Me wish go fun-fest. Me wish dunk prince."

"Heartfelt wish is true wish," growled a gruff voice. "And so, you go."

Rrrrrella spun around. She was staring at a bear, the very one she had given fish.

"Who you?" she asked.

"Me your beary godfather."

Rrrrrella was overjoyed—then underjoyed.

She mumbled, "Me got no bark-clogs, to keep on log. Feets too big."

"No be bugbrain," snorted her godfather. He swiped the air with a paw, and, instantly, an enormous pair of clogs appeared.

Rrrrrella tried them on. They fit perfectly.

Then the grizzly waved a paw over her and—*poof*—the wildflowers she wore were dust. He patted and matted her fur, and it tangled like the very forest floor.

She boomed, "THANKS!" and gave him a crunching hug.

"Be back sundown!" he warned. "Or you be like sisters make
you. No furry and smelly. But plenty flowery."

Rrrrrella wasn't worried. She had lots of time. She skipped
off, shaking the whole forest as she went.

At the fun-fest, there were Bigfoot women from every clan. The games had begun. One by one the women leaped onto a log where the prince crouched, ready. One by one he dumped them into the water.

Rrrrrella's stepsisters hated games. But to catch the prince they'd do anything—even give logs a twirl. And they hoped a good drenching might even wash off his stench. But they never got the chance. When their turn came, the prince saw their wildflower-chains and glowered. He tossed them in the water, snarling, *"NO PICK FLOWERS!"*

The day grew late. Everyone had tried to win. Everyone had failed.

The Bigfoot prince rumbled, *"Rrrrrats! No brrrrride!"* He was about to slouch home when—THUNK!—Rrrrrella bounded onto the log, pounding her chest and whooping, "ME DUNK PRINCE!"

Grunting with all her might, she spun the log like a big twig. Then she gave it a twist and—*floop!*—the prince flopped into the river.

There was a stunned silence. The Bigfoots were slow-witted, so it took them a while to figure out what had happened. When at last they began to chant, *"Brrrrride! Brrrrride! Brrrrride!"* the sun was setting!

Rrrrrella saw that and rushed into the dense trees, shrieking, "EEEEEK!" just as her matted fur went sleek and wildflowers began to sprout.

The prince lurched from the water, dripping and crushed. His dream woman—shaggy as the forest floor, smelly as a fish, and strong—was gone.

Scratching his craggy head, he slumped down on a boulder. *"Drrrrrat! Drrrrrat! Drrrrrat!"* He gnashed his mossy teeth. *"Where my stinking beauty go?"*

Then he saw one big bark clog. Hers! Now perhaps he *could* find his princess.

The prince shuffled from snag to snag, cave to cave, lugging the lost clog. But though all the Bigfoot women tried it on, it was too large for anyone.

The moment he reached Rrrrrella's cave, her stepmother and stepsisters pounced on the prince, wrestled the clog from him, and jumped into it eagerly. Their feet were so small, they all fit at once!

Then Rrrrrella bounded up, yelling, "Me trrrrry! Me trrrrry! ME! ME! ME!"

She did. And her foot fit the clog like a seed in a pod.

When she pulled out its mate, the Bigfoot prince knew he'd found his bride. He thumped his chest and roared with joy.

The stepsisters roared too. In tantrums, they yanked up some wildflowers and saplings. Their mother kicked the prince black and blue.

Soon there was a rowdy wedding in the old-growth forest.
Everyone was invited. Even Rrrrrella's stepmother and stepsisters
could come—if they followed these rules carefully:
   No *pick flower.*
   No *pull tree.*
   No *kick royal family.*